The Owl and the Turtle

Written and illustrated by Carol Drew Eckstrom

The Owl and the Turtle

Carol Drew Eckstrom

Published by:
Wolf Grove Media, LLC
Bothell, WA USA

ISBN-10: 958329-06-1

ISBN-13: 978-1-958329-06-1

Dedicated to Owl

With love, Turtle

I know you've
heard the story of
the tortoise and the hare.

Well, here's a little
story of a less
familiar pair.

The owl and the turtle
went out one day to walk,
and as they went along
their way,

they talked and
talked and talked.

They talked of things they
liked to do and things
they'd never done.

They talked of things
that scared them,

and things they thought
were fun.

Before too long the owl tired, his feet weren't made for walking.

"Hop on my back,"
the turtle said.
"That way we'll keep
on talking."

They continued walking, night overcame the day. The turtle became frightened as he could not see the way.

"Do not be afraid," said Owl. "For I will be your sight owls hunt and see their best when daytime turns to night."

Together they became as one
with common eyes and feet.

Together they could conquer

what alone would bring defeat.

The owl and the turtle are good friends as you can tell.
PARK

It matters not to them that one
has feathers, one a shell.

For friends are friends in good times and when problems arise. They share their thoughts and troubles, and sometimes feet and eyes!

www.ingramcontent.com/pod-product-compliance
Lightning Source LLC
Chambersburg PA
CBHW041923180726
48295CB00002B/55